The
THANKSGIVING
MYSTERY

By Gail Herman
Illustrated by Duendes del Sur

SCHOLASTIC INC.

New York   Toronto   London   Auckland   Sydney
Mexico City   New Delhi   Hong Kong   Buenos Aires

ISBN 0-439-78359-3

Illustrations by Duendes del Sur

12 11 10 9 8 7 6 5   8 9/0

Printed in the U.S.A.
First printing, November 2005

Scooby-Doo, Shaggy, and the gang were getting ready for their Thanksgiving dinner.

"First things first," Velma said. "We have to get food."

"Like, yeah," Shaggy agreed. "So, what are we doing here?"

FARMER GREEN'S FARM

"We're getting fresh vegetables from the farm," Daphne said.

"Regetables?" Scooby made a face.

"Come on, good buddy," Shaggy whispered. "Maybe there's a pizza place close by."

Excited, Fred, Daphne, and Velma jumped out of the Mystery Machine. Shaggy and Scooby moved s-l-o-w-l-y, s-l-o-w-l-y until . . .

"That sounds like fun," Velma said.
"But the contest is on the other side of the farm," Daphne added. "Down that big hill, past all the pumpkin patches and vegetable gardens."
"Let's pick our vegetables first," suggested Fred.

Fred, Velma, and Daphne looked at the lettuce and squash.

"Like, let's get a move on," Shaggy grumbled. "We've been doing this for *five* minutes already."

Finally, Shaggy nudged Velma. "Ahhhh!" he screamed.

"Rahhh!" Scooby echoed. Velma had disappeared. In her place stood a spooky pumpkinhead monster!

"Velma!" cried Shaggy. "What's happened to you?"

The pumpkinhead didn't answer. It reached out one stiff arm. . . .

Shaggy grabbed Scooby. Scooby grabbed Shaggy.

"Relp!" cried Scooby.

"Help is right!" said Shaggy.

They raced over to Fred.

But Fred was gone.
"He's turned into a pumpkinhead! Just like Velma!" Shaggy yelled.

"Raphne!" Scooby yelped.
But Daphne had changed into a pumpkinhead, too.

The pumpkinheads swayed closer. Their arms stretched out toward Shaggy and Scooby, twisting and reaching.

Scooby and Shaggy ran. Vines wrapped around their arms. Garden hoses wound around their legs.

"Zoinks!" cried Shaggy. "Everything's alive!"

Finally, the two friends tripped—right into a pumpkin patch!

In a flash, they leaped to their feet.
"What's happening?" Shaggy groaned,
confused. His voice sounded strange, hollow.
Then he looked at Scooby and screamed.

Scooby pointed at Shaggy and howled. They'd been turned into pumpkinhead monsters, too!

The buddies tumbled and stumbled and rolled down the hill.

"Farmhouse, here we come!" Shaggy shouted.

Crash! They landed on a long table. From opposite ends, they slid across the top of it.
   Splat!
   They stopped.

Scooby and Shaggy were scared. They
were frightened. They were hungry. They
gulped down pie, after pie, after pie.

20

At last, they staggered to their feet. "We've got an audience, Scoob, old pal," said Shaggy.

"Raphne! Relma! Red!" said Scooby.

"You've been turned back into humans!" said Shaggy.

"One minute you guys were standing by the vegetables," Shaggy explained, "and the next minute, horrible pumpkinhead monsters were there instead."

Velma laughed.

"Those pumpkinheads were always there!"

Velma went on. "You just didn't see them because Fred, Daphne, and I were standing in front of them! Farmer Green needed us to judge the pie eating contest, so we had to leave the vegetable patch right away. There was no time to explain, until now."

"It must have seemed like we disappeared," said Daphne, "and that the pumpkinheads took our places!"

"But they were reaching for us!" Shaggy protested.

Velma shook her head. "It's very windy today. The wind must have moved the pumpkinheads' arms."

"What about those vines and hoses?" asked Shaggy. "They tried to grab us, too."

Velma sighed. "You ran so fast, you were tripping," she said. "It was all your imagination, guys."

"Oh, yeah?" Shaggy asked again. He knocked on his pumpkinhead. "Like, is this my imagination, too?"

Fred pulled the pumpkin off Shaggy. "You must have fallen," said Velma, "right into these jack-o-lanterns."

"Yeah, yeah," said Shaggy. Now that he thought about it, he and Scooby did take a nasty tumble into the pumpkin patch. "Thanks and all," he continued, "but who won the pie eating contest?"

"You guys did, of course!" said Daphne. "And here comes the prize!"

All at once, Scooby's eyes widened in fear. Shaggy turned pale. "It's another pumpkinhead monster! For real!" Shaggy yelled.

He and Scooby ran away as fast as they could.

"Wait!" Daphne called after them. "It's only Farmer Green. He's holding your prize, a giant pumpkin!"

29

Shaggy and Scooby were already down the road . . . running across the street . . . around the corner . . . and right into a pizza stand!

"Finally!" said Shaggy. "Thanksgiving dinner."

"Rappy Ranksgiving!"